Bluebell Woods

Evie's Secret Hideaway

For my daughter Elizabeth Norton,
a fellow writer, whose success inspired
me to keep trying! Thanks, Beth X
L.N.

For Iolo, love Mummy X
R.H.

STRIPES PUBLISHING
An imprint of Magi Publications
1 The Coda Centre, 189 Munster Road,
London SW6 6AW

A paperback original
First published in Great Britain in 2011

ISBN: 978-1-84715-194-0

A CIP catalogue record for this book is available
from the British Library.

Printed and bound in China.

STP/1800/0003/0511

10 9 8 7 6 5 4 3 2 1

Bluebell Woods

Evie's Secret Hideaway

Liss Norton

Illustrated by Rebecca Harry

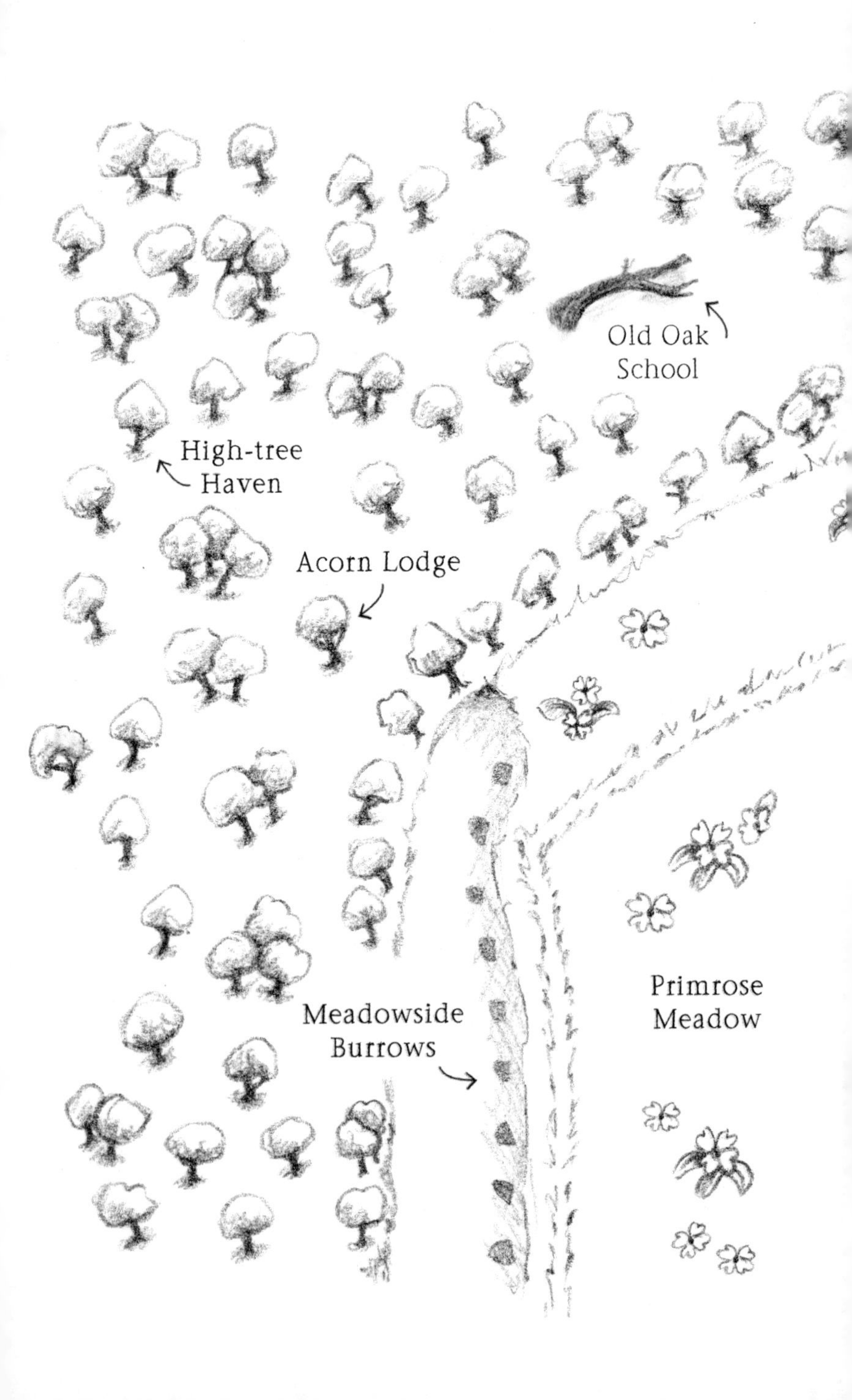
Old Oak
School
High-tree
Haven
Acorn Lodge
Meadowside
Burrows
Primrose
Meadow

Evie grabbed a walnut from the pile in front of her, cracked the shell with her sharp teeth and let the kernel drop into the bowl in the middle of the table.

They worked quickly, though Evie made sure she was always one walnut behind Reggie.

Reggie dropped his last empty nutshell on the table. "I win!" he cheered.

"Well done," said Evie. She opened her last nut, then picked up the bowl. "Where shall I put them, Grandad?"

"That was quick!" said Grandad. "How about in the larder? Next to that bramble jelly you brought." He licked his lips. "I'm looking forward to that. Your mum's jellies are the best."

"I like Mum's hazelnut spread better," said Reggie. "But we haven't found many hazelnuts this year."

"Ah," said Grandad. "I know just the place for hazelnuts. All the squirrels for miles around used to go there in the autumn when I was young."

"Where is it?" asked Evie eagerly. She loved exploring parts of Bluebell Woods that she'd never been to before.

"I'll draw you a map," said Grandad. He fetched some charcoal and a piece of bark-paper, and began to draw. "There," he said. "It's a fair old distance. Cross the

Stepping Stones, head south-east, then just follow the map."

"Thanks, Grandad," said Evie. "I'll get my friends to go there next time we go foraging."

Grandad winked at Reggie. "If your mum's making hazelnut spread, put me down for a jar." The kettle started to whistle, but just as Grandad was about to get up to make the tea, they heard footsteps on the spiral stairs leading up to the drey, followed by a knock at the door.

"Can we come in?" a voice called.

"That's Honey," said Evie. She ran along the hall and opened the front door. Her friends Honey, Natalie, and Florence crowded inside.

"What a wind!" cried Honey, smoothing her ruffled fur. "It nearly blew me away."

"It's not that bad!" Natalie laughed.

"Your mum said you were here. We're going foraging – do you want to come?" said Florence.

"You bet!" Evie exclaimed. She took her friends into the living room. "Hello, Mr Morningdew. Hi, Reggie," they chorused.

"Hello, girls. What are you up to today?" asked Grandad.

"We're off foraging," said Evie. She rolled up the map, pulled on her coat, then took the basket Florence had brought for her. "See you later, Reggie." She kissed his furry cheek. "Bye, Grandad."

"Can I come?" said Reggie.

"I think Evie's planning to go a long way," Grandad told him. "And it's a bit far for you, Reggie. Anyway, you and I are going to make walnut biscuits."

"I love walnut biscuits!" said Reggie, his fluffy tail twitching excitedly.

"Me, too," said Grandad. "So let's get started."

Evie and her friends hurried outside. The wind tugged at their coats and buffeted them as they ran down the stairs.

"What have you got there?" asked Florence, as they crossed Primrose Meadow.

"A map to a hazel grove my grandad used to go to," said Evie. "Loads of squirrels met up there in autumn and… Whoa, look out!" A large crab apple was rolling towards them.

They jumped aside. Monty Hornbeam, a shrew who went to their school, was racing after it. "Sorry," he called. "The wind's behind it and I can't make it stop."

"Where did you find it, Monty?" Natalie called after him.

"The crab apple tree near the school, but I'm pretty sure it's the last one."

"Shame," sighed Natalie. "I could have made crab apple jelly."

"You'll have to make something with hazelnuts instead," Honey said. "How far is it to this grove, Evie? Didn't your grandad say something about it being a long way?"

"Quite a way," Evie replied. "But it'll be an adventure, going into a part of the woods that we don't know."

Honey wrinkled her nose. "Can't we forage closer to home today? It's chilly and I think it'll rain later."

"A bit of rain won't hurt," said Evie. "And we'll soon warm up if we walk quickly. Anyway, I want to pick some nuts for Reggie. He needs cheering up."

"How come?" asked Natalie.

"He's been really fed up since the Brambles moved away. Oscar was his best friend."

"Poor Reggie," said Florence. "I'd hate it if one of you moved away."

"Me, too," Evie agreed. "So I want to try and find him a new best friend."

"We'll help," Honey offered.

"There's my cousin Billy," Florence said. "But he won't start school till next term so he's a bit younger than Reggie."

"That's the trouble," sighed Evie. "There aren't any boys the same age as Reggie in Bluebell Woods."

"It'll have to be someone older or younger then," Natalie said thoughtfully.

"Monty's too old," said Florence.

"And so is Johnny," said Evie. "I'm sure we'll think of someone. But for now let's concentrate on finding food. That hazel grove sounds—"

"I'm not walking for miles," Honey interrupted. "Especially as there might not even be any nuts. If loads of squirrels go there they might have picked the trees clean already."

"We won't know unless we go," said Evie.

"Let's forage as we go along," suggested Natalie, hoping to prevent an argument.

"If we can't find food around here, we can go to Evie's grove."

"That sounds fair," said Florence.

"OK… I suppose," Honey agreed.

Evie sighed. She could see that Natalie's plan made sense, but she was itching to explore the new hazel grove.

They reached the Stepping Stones that crossed the Babbling Brook and skipped over to the other side.

"There's a Hazelgrove!" Florence giggled. "But not the one we want." Mr Hazelgrove, their teacher, was examining fungi on a fallen branch.

"He's got his back to us," whispered Evie. "Let's sneak past." She was behind with her homework and she didn't want him sending her home to finish it.

The friends crept by, but it wasn't easy to walk quietly with the ground deep in crisp, fallen leaves.

Once Mr Hazelgrove was out of sight, they started searching for food. Florence and Natalie delved into heaps of fallen leaves while Honey and Evie climbed up into the trees. It was so late in the season that every larder in Bluebell Woods was full to bursting and there was little left to be found.

Honey climbed down from a tree where she'd been searching for beech masts. "Nothing," she said glumly.

"It looks like we'll have to try your hazel grove then, Evie," said Florence.

"Brilliant!" Evie unrolled the map. "We have to go south-east until we come to a thicket of holly trees, then go up a slope.

The hazel trees are at the top." She set off along a narrow path that seemed to be heading in the right direction. "Come on," she called. "If we hurry, we'll easily be back before dark." She beamed at her friends. "This could be a real adventure."

As the friends walked along the woodland path, swinging their baskets, birds flitted from branch to branch and golden leaves danced on the wind.

"Are we going the right way?" Honey asked, after a while. "We seem to be heading back the way we came."

Evie looked at the map. "Oh dear," she said. "I didn't notice that the path forks. We must have gone right instead of left."

They retraced their steps and soon came to the path they needed. It was overgrown and they found themselves walking under gloomy tunnels of arching brambles, hung thickly with cobwebs. "No wonder we missed it," Florence said. "I shouldn't think anyone's been along here for years."

Natalie shivered. "I don't like it here," she said. "It feels spooky being all closed in and… What was that?"

A bush beside the path rustled. They stopped and stared at it, ready to run. Evie's heart pounded furiously. Honey gripped her paw tightly. "It's just the wind," Florence quavered. "Isn't it?"

A large moth fluttered out from under a leaf. Honey jumped back, catching her coat on a bramble. "Aagh!" she shrieked. "Something's got me!"

"It's only a thorn, Honey!" Evie laughed, unhooking her.

They set off again and finally came out of the bramble tunnel into an area filled with glossy-leaved holly trees. "The holly thicket," Evie said, checking the map. "We're almost there!"

They hurried through the holly trees and up the slope. "At last," Honey said, as they reached the hazel grove.

"Grandad was right," said Evie, gazing at the trees. "There must be thousands of nuts here." Springing up into a tree, she leaped from branch to branch so the nuts showered down.

Florence, Natalie and Honey scurried to catch them in their baskets, and very soon they'd filled them to the brim.

"Perhaps it was worth the long walk after all," Honey said, as they set off home.

"Hang on," said Natalie. "There's a hawthorn tree." She picked a ruby-red leaf from a low branch and put it into her basket. "They're so colourful in autumn, I could use them to make some pictures."

They helped her find more leaves, then set off again, but they hadn't gone far before the sky began to darken.

"It's going to rain," Florence warned.

"I told you!" groaned Honey. "We'll get drenched."

The friends sped up, but they still hadn't reached the Stepping Stones when the first drops of rain began to fall. "If you hadn't made us come all this way, Evie, we could have run home and stayed dry," Honey complained.

"But then we wouldn't have filled our baskets," replied Evie. "And it's only a bit of rain."

Lightning fizzed across the sky, followed by a deafening crack of thunder. Natalie screamed.

Florence grabbed her paw. "Don't be scared, Nat," she said.

"Let's find shelter," Honey gasped, as the rain began to pour down.

"This way," cried Evie, raising her voice to make herself heard above the pounding of the rain.

They dived off the path, which was already becoming muddy, and darted through the undergrowth. At last, they came upon an ash tree whose trunk and knobbly, jutting roots offered a little protection. Shivering, they crouched down close to the trunk.

Florence slipped an arm round Natalie's trembling shoulders as the thunder boomed. "It'll be over soon, Nat," she said. "Storms never last long."

"I hope you're right," quavered Natalie.

As another bolt of lightning streaked across the sky, Evie spotted a dark hole near the base of the tree trunk. Peering inside, she found a tunnel leading upwards.

"I wonder where this goes," Evie said, crawling inside.

"What are you doing?" asked Florence.

"Exploring," she replied. "Back in a minute."

The tunnel sloped steeply up inside the tree trunk, and soon Evie could see a rough circle of grey light ahead. As she crawled eagerly towards it, another flash of lightning lit up the tunnel. Now she could see that the circle of light was an opening into a big chamber.

"A secret room," she gasped.

She crawled through the opening into a hollow right inside the tree. A narrow crack in the trunk let in enough light for her to see that the hollow was big enough to shelter all of them. "Hey!" she called excitedly. "Come up here." Her voice echoed eerily.

"Where are you?" Honey called back.

"Follow the tunnel," Evie said. There was another clap of thunder. As the rumbles died away, she heard scampering in the tunnel, then Honey appeared, followed by Natalie and Florence.

"We'll keep dry in here all right!" exclaimed Honey, gazing at the solid walls.

"Anyone fancy a picnic?" Evie asked.

Her friends stared at her, confused.

"A hazelnut picnic," she explained. She darted down the tunnel and returned moments later with her foraging basket. "Help yourselves," she said, setting it down in the middle of the floor.

"I'm going to dry my fur first," Honey said. "It's soaked." A few dried leaves lay scattered on the floor. "These will do as towels." They rubbed their fur dry, then sat in a circle and nibbled hazelnuts.

The storm slowly moved away, until the thunder was nothing more than a low rumble in the distance. "Shall we see if the rain's stopped?" suggested Florence. "If it has, we ought to go home. It must be getting late."

They crawled back down the tunnel. The sky was lighter now and the rain was nothing more than drizzle. "Hey, I know this part of the woods," said Evie, looking around. "We're near the Babbling Brook."

"There it is!" exclaimed Florence. She ran towards the Stepping Stones, then stopped in dismay.

"What's wrong?" asked Natalie.

"The Babbling Brook's risen with all that rain," Florence gasped. The water, which normally trickled lazily along, was rushing by. "We can't reach the first stone. How are we going to get back across?"

Chapter Three

"What are we going to do?" wailed Honey. Her eyes widened with horror. "What if we can't get home for days?"

"Of course we can get home," said Evie. "And this is a real adventure."

"I don't want an adventure!" Honey snapped, stamping her foot hard. The movement made her lose her balance and she slipped over in the mud.

"Look at me!" Honey spluttered, as her friends helped her to her feet. "I'm filthy!"

"Let me help," said Natalie, taking out

her hankie and wiping Honey's face clean. "How are we going to cross the brook, Evie?"

"We need a long twig that will reach from the bank to the first stepping stone," explained Evie. "You stay and help Honey, Nat. Me and Florence will search for one."

She and Florence scampered away. They looked amongst the fallen leaves and arching blackberry canes. "Here's one," Florence called, at last. It was a long, fairly straight twig with a few brown leaves still clinging to it.

"Perfect," said Evie. "Let's see if we can lift it." The twig was heavy, but they managed to carry it between them.

Natalie and Evie were waiting for them by the water's edge. "Give us a hand," Evie cried. She and Florence let the twig drop, then the four of them pushed it out over the water until one end rested on the first stone.

"It doesn't look very safe," Honey said doubtfully.

"I'll try it out," said Evie. Picking up her basket of hazelnuts, she ran across the branch to the first stepping stone. "It's as solid as anything," she called. "Come on."

One by one, they walked along the twig, then jumped across the Stepping Stones. "Made it!" said Florence, as she reached the other side. "That was a great idea, Evie."

It was almost dark now and they hurried towards Hedge End where Honey lived. As they drew near, Harvey and Albie appeared.

"There you are," said Albie crossly. "Mum and Dad made us come and look for you, Honey." He raised his voice. "Dad, she's over here!"

Harvey came closer, then started to laugh. "Have you been having a mud fight, Honey?" he hooted.

"Of course not!" Honey glared at him, then flounced past with her nose in the air. Her friends followed.

"So Honey's been playing proper games for once, instead of doing girly dancing!" Harvey laughed.

"Why did I have to have brothers?" Honey complained. "Everywhere I go, they're there, being horrible."

Mr Pennyroyal came running towards them. "Where have you been, Honey?" he demanded. "We've been worried sick." His eyes widened as he took in Honey's mud-splattered clothes.

Evie quickly explained about the Stepping Stones and how Honey had slipped over.

"You're all safe and sound now," said Mr Pennyroyal. "That's the main thing. But you should get off home. Your parents must be wondering what's become of you. And you need a good wash, Honey."

The friends said goodbye and Evie scampered home across Primrose Meadow. She couldn't help feeling sorry for Honey.

It must be a pain having brothers like Harvey and Albie, especially when all they did was play tricks and poke fun at Honey.

She felt a sudden twinge of guilt, remembering her own brother, Reggie. Not that he was a pest like Harvey and Albie – she loved him to bits – but since Oscar had moved away he wanted to spend all his time with her, and she'd have liked to have a bit more time with just her friends.

What we need is a secret place, Evie thought. *A place that nobody else knows about, where we can go to be by ourselves*. Suddenly she knew where that place was – the hollow tree where they'd sheltered from the storm. It would make the perfect secret den!

Chapter Four

"I wonder what Oscar's doing now," Reggie sighed, as he and Evie walked to school next morning.

"He's probably on his way to school, like us," said Evie brightly. She squeezed Reggie's paw. "You won't always feel this sad, you know."

"I will," said Reggie miserably. "I'll never be happy again without Oscar."

Florence came skipping along the path outside Meadowside Burrows. "Hi, you two," she called, catching them up.

"Hi, Florence," Evie called back. She was desperate to tell Florence her idea about the secret den, but she didn't want Reggie to hear. She'd have to wait until playtime.

At break Evie dashed out of the classroom. "Quick!" she called to her friends. "I've got something to tell you."

They hurried after Evie to the far end of the playground where three birch trees grew close together.

Checking that nobody was about, Evie pulled them behind one of the trees. "I've had a brilliant idea," she whispered. "We should make the hollow tree into our secret den."

"That would be fantastic!" Florence cried. "We could take some games there."

Honey clapped her paws delightedly. "I'd be able to get away from Harvey and Albie," she said.

"I made those hawthorn leaf pictures last night," said Natalie. "We could hang them up in the den to make it cosy."

"Great idea!" said Evie. "Let's go there after school today and work out what needs to be done." She peeped out from behind the tree to make sure nobody was coming and spotted Reggie all alone on the far side of the playground, bouncing a ball. "Oh dear," she sighed.

"What's wrong?" asked Natalie.

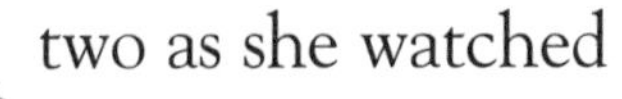

"Nothing," said Evie. She felt torn in two as she watched Reggie. She could see that he needed someone to play with, but she wanted to spend time with her friends, planning the den. As she turned back to her friends, she felt horribly guilty for choosing them over her little brother.

"In this afternoon's lesson we'll learn how to build up useful stores in autumn," announced Mr Hazelgrove. "We all know about turning over fallen leaves to find apples and nuts. We might find conkers there, too, which can be used to make stain remover." He pointed to his desk, which was piled high with conkers in their prickly cases. "I want you to work in groups to find the best way of opening a conker case."

Honey turned round and grinned at her friends. They all loved group work because it gave them the chance to sit together.

They sat at the back of the class as Mr Hazelgrove handed out the conkers. "I always prick my paws on conkers," complained Honey.

"They're handy when they're open, though," Natalie pointed out. "My dad washes our sheets in water that's had smashed up conkers soaked in it. It gets them really clean." She glanced round the room. "Who's Reggie working with?"

"Sophie and Monty," Evie said. "I checked, in case he needed to join our group." She turned the conker over.

"Shall I try opening it first?" She began to search the conker case for a weak spot. Her face suddenly brightened. "Hey, we could make a swing at the den!" she said.

Florence and Natalie leaned forward, eager to hear more.

"We could make it out of honeysuckle stems with a twig to sit on and—"

"Tell us later, Evie," Honey whispered. "Mr Hazelgrove might hear."

"And we could loop it up in the tree when we're not there," continued Evie, ignoring her. "So nobody… Ouch!" She jerked her paw back. "These conker spikes are really sharp."

To her horror, she noticed Mr Hazelgrove standing behind Florence. "The lesson is about conkers, not swings, girls," he said crossly.

"Sorry, sir," the friends said.

They went back to their work, but Evie could hardly sit still for thinking about all the wonderful things they'd do in their den. "Just think, our very own secret hideaway!" she whispered. "We can have picnics and nobody will know where we are."

"Evie," warned Florence. "You'll get us into trouble again."

By the time the lesson ended, their conker case was still in one piece. Mr Hazelgrove tutted as he collected it. "You haven't got far, girls."

"It's so prickly," said Honey. She didn't want him to know that they'd hardly spent any time trying to open it.

They returned to their places and began packing their school bags, ready to go home. Mr Hazelgrove sat down at his desk. "I've been checking the homework," he said. "Where's yours, Evie?"

"Um… I haven't quite finished it yet."

"Everyone else managed to do it," Mr Hazelgrove said sternly.

"Sorry, sir. I'll bring it in tomorrow."

"You can stay behind and do it now."

Evie stared at him, aghast. "Not today, Mr Hazelgrove, please," she begged.

She wouldn't be able to go to the den and do all the things she'd planned!

"You know how important homework is. You'll stay here until it's done," said Mr Hazelgrove. He dismissed the rest of the class, while Evie sat slumped at her desk.

Natalie, Florence and Honey came over. "Bad luck, Evie," said Florence.

"You'll have to go without me," Evie sighed, taking her homework out of her bag. "Tell me all about it tomorrow."

"We can't go to the den without Evie," said Natalie, as she, Florence and Honey walked home from school.

"I agree," said Florence. "But it's a shame. I was really looking forward to setting it up."

"Me, too," Honey agreed in a gloomy voice.

"I'm going home to tidy my bedroom," said Natalie. "My mum keeps going on at me about it."

"Do you want a hand?" asked Honey.

"Yes, please," said Natalie.

The three of them scampered to Blackberry Snug and headed straight for Natalie's room. "I'm not surprised your mum's been going on about it!" Honey giggled.

Art materials were scattered across the floor and there were piles of clean clothes waiting to be put away in the drawers.

"I know it's bad," sighed Natalie. "But I hate tidying." She held up two leaf pictures. "These are the pictures I made last night. Do you think they'll do for the den?"

"They're great," said Florence. She picked up a paintbrush and put it in Natalie's paintbox. "Have you got anything else we could take?"

"There's this rug," said Natalie. She reached under her bed and pulled out a rug made from woven grass. "I made it a couple of months ago, but then I didn't know what to do with it. We've already got loads of rugs."

"Just what we need," said Honey.

They worked busily, tidying up and sorting out games to take to the den.

"Do we want beanbags?" Natalie asked, as she put her art box away in a cupboard. "Mr Bramble gave my dad two beanbags when they moved to Campion Forest."

"Don't you want them?" asked Florence.

"No, they made the living room feel cramped so Mum put them in the storeroom."

They hurriedly put away the last of Natalie's clothes, then ran down the passage to the storeroom. The beanbag covers were knitted in colourful stripes.

"These are perfect," Florence said. "They're big enough to share, too."

"I can't wait to show everything to Evie," said Honey. "She's going to love all this stuff."

Straight after school next day, the friends headed for their den. Evie was thrilled to see the things they'd sorted out at Natalie's. They took everything, together with a skipping rope and a lantern supplied by

Florence, a biscuit tin from Evie, and Honey's pine cone collection. They'd packed most of it into their foraging baskets and hoped to head on to the Hazel Grove to collect more hazelnuts later.

"Let's ask Mr Willowherb to take us across the Babbling Brook," said Florence. "We'll never carry all this across the Stepping Stones."

Mr Willowherb was sweeping his raft. "Hello, girls," he said. "Do you want a ride?"

"Yes, please," they chorused.

"Hop aboard then." They jumped on to the raft, and Mr Willowherb pushed off from the bank.

"Where are you off to with all this?" he asked.

"Nowhere," said Natalie, flustered. "I mean ... nowhere special."

Mr Willowherb winked at them. "A secret, is it?"

The friends exchanged glances.

"Don't worry, I won't tell." Mr Willowherb steered the raft towards the bank. "I had a secret den over here when I was about your age."

"That must have been fun," said Evie. "I wish we had one."

Mr Willowherb winked again. "I bet you do!"

"He knows we've got a den!" Honey said, once they'd stepped ashore and the ferryman had punted away.

"But he doesn't know where it is," Florence pointed out.

"Suppose he tells someone, though," groaned Honey. "Harvey and Albie will find out and—"

"Calm down, Honey," said Natalie. "Mr Willowherb doesn't know for sure that we've got a den. And even if he does, he said he won't tell."

They hurried to the den and crawled inside. Evie lit the lantern.

"It's a bit dusty in here," said Natalie. "I'll find a fir twig and sweep it out."

"I'll hang the pictures," said Florence, "and make a shelf for your pine cone collection, Honey."

"Shall we make the swing, Honey?" Evie asked. "It'll be quicker with two."

Soon the den was perfect. The colourful beanbags, pictures and rug made it look homely. The games were piled up on one side with the biscuit tin on top. Honey's pine cone collection was arranged on a shelf woven from twigs.

Outside, the swing hung beside the den's entrance. The honeysuckle stem ropes were securely tied to a high branch and the seat was made from a fat twig. The friends took turns on it, shrieking with laughter as they swooped to and fro.

"We should go and collect some hazelnuts," said Florence, when they'd all had a go. "It'll be dark soon."

"Shame," Evie sighed. She bounded up the tree trunk, pulled up the swing and wrapped it round a branch. "There. No one will spot that," she said, racing down again.

Suddenly, they heard someone coming. Evie ran to the den's entrance and stood in front, fluffing up her tail to hide it.

Harvey and Albie appeared round the corner. "What are you doing?" Albie asked, his eyes narrowing suspiciously.

The friends exchanged anxious glances. "We're going foraging, if you must know," said Honey.

"Funny place for foraging," Albie said. "That's an ash tree. You won't find any nuts there."

"We stopped for a rest," said Florence. She held out her basket to the boys. "Do you want to help?"

"Not likely!" snorted Harvey. He and Albie ran off into the woods.

"That was close," Honey gasped. "Quick thinking, Evie, spreading your tail out like that."

"Why don't we hide the opening?" suggested Natalie.

They gathered twigs, and arranged them over the entrance, leaving an opening just big enough to crawl through.

"There," said Honey. "Nobody will find the way in now."

"We'll have to remember where our tree is," joked Evie, "or we might not be able to find it, either."

Picking up their foraging baskets, they set off for the Hazel Grove.

"We should have a sleepover at the den!" exclaimed Florence. "On Saturday night, to celebrate finishing it."

"Oh, yes!" cried Evie. She couldn't think of anything better.

"Great idea!" said Honey and Natalie.

As soon as they reached the Hazel Grove, they started quickly filling their baskets. Suddenly, a young squirrel jumped down from a tree, landing next to Evie. "Hello," he said.

"Hello," said Evie. "What's your name?"

"Peter Morningdew."

"Morningdew?" the friends chorused, astonished.

"Yes. What's wrong with that?"

"Nothing," Evie said. "It's just … my name's Morningdew, too. Evie Morningdew."

The squirrel stared at her, open-mouthed.

"Perhaps we're related," said Evie eagerly. It would be amazing to find relations she knew nothing about.

There was a movement in the tree above their heads. Then two grown-up squirrels sprang down beside them. "Good afternoon," they said.

"Mum, Dad, this is Evie Morningdew," said Peter excitedly.

"Well I never!" gasped Peter's dad. "I'm Wilbur and this is my wife, Alice. Tell me about your family. I think we might be cousins."

"I've got a little brother called Reggie," Evie began. "He must be around the same age as Peter. My dad's called Rufus and my mum's called Harriet. My grandad's name is Larry—"

"Larry Morningdew!" exclaimed Wilbur. "I've heard my dad talk about a cousin Larry. He married a squirrel called Millie and moved to her village."

"Millie was my gran's name!" cried Evie.

"We live just beyond the Hazel Grove. Do you live round here?" asked Alice.

"We live in the village near Primrose Meadow. These are my friends." Evie introduced them.

"Tell us about your village," said Peter eagerly. "I've never been anywhere except our part of the woods."

"It's fantastic!" said Evie. "Lots of animals live there and everyone's so friendly. We have a wonderful summer ball. Oh, and school is amazing! We learn so much from our brilliant teacher, Mr Hazelgrove!"

Florence, Honey and Natalie stared at her in astonishment. Evie wasn't normally that keen on school.

Alice sighed. "That's the trouble with living out in the woods," she said. "There's no school for Peter to go to. Wilbur and I have to teach him at home." She stroked his ears. "I worry about him missing out."

"Why don't you come back with us?" said Evie hopefully. "You could meet my mum and dad and brother Reggie."

"We can't right now, but thank you. We're too busy foraging for the winter," said Wilbur. "But we'd love to come some other time. Nice to meet you all." He, Alice and Peter darted up a tree and disappeared amongst the branches.

"What was all that about?" Honey demanded when they'd gone. "School's amazing? Mr Hazelgrove's a brilliant teacher?"

"Peter's about the same age as Reggie," said Evie excitedly. "If they like the sound of the village, they might move there. Then Reggie will have a new friend."

"Good thinking," said Florence.

Natalie glanced up at the sky. It was already starting to get dark. "We should go home," she said. "Or our parents will worry again."

They headed for the Stepping Stones, pausing briefly near their den to check that the entrance was properly camouflaged.

"You can hardly see it," Evie said approvingly.

"Oh!" squeaked Honey, all of a sudden. "What's happened to my nuts?" Her basket was almost empty. "I thought it felt light."

Natalie turned the basket over. "There's a hole," she said. They looked back along the path and saw a trail of nuts leading off into the distance.

"I'm not going all the way back to pick them up!" Honey said crossly.

"You can share mine," said Natalie. "Come on, let's get home."

Evie thought about the other Morningdew family as they hurried along. She wouldn't tell her parents about them yet; she didn't want to get Reggie's hopes up about Peter becoming his new friend. But things were definitely looking promising.

Chapter Six

"Mum," said Evie the next morning, while Reggie was in his bedroom packing his school bag. "Me and my friends have made a secret den in the woods. Can we have a sleepover there on Saturday night?" She didn't like telling her mum about the den when it was supposed to be a secret, but how else could she ask for permission?

"I don't see why not. Shall I bake some hazelnut cookies for you to take?"

Evie hugged her. "Thanks, Mum. That'll be brilliant!"

Reggie came into the kitchen. "I don't want to go to school," he said sadly.

"Oh, Reggie." Mum put her arm round him. "I'm afraid you have to, darling."

Reggie began to cry.

"We'll take you to Campion Forest to visit Oscar when the spring comes," promised Mum.

"I want to go now," sobbed Reggie.

Evie took his paw. "Let's play tag."

Mum dried Reggie's eyes. "You can have a game while I make breakfast."

Dad came in. "Games before breakfast?" he said. "That sounds like fun."

"Reggie and Evie are going to play tag," said Mum.

"Count me in!" Dad exclaimed. He picked Reggie up. "Come on, I bet we catch Evie!" He ran towards her. "Watch out for the Dad-and-Reggie-monster!"

Grabbing her coat, Evie raced outside. Dad and Reggie followed. By the time they reached the bottom of the steps, Reggie was giggling and shouting to be put down.

Dad set him on his feet. "Thanks, Evie," he mouthed, as Reggie charged towards her, laughing.

It was a breezy morning and they played amongst the whirling leaves. At last, Mum called them for breakfast and they darted inside, hungry after all the running about.

"Eat up quickly," said Mum, setting down bowls of steaming porridge. "You don't want to be late for school."

To Evie's relief, Reggie didn't say anything more about not going to school. *If only the other Morningdews decide to move here*, she thought. She hoped she'd said enough to persuade them.

"I can stay at the den on Saturday night," said Florence at playtime.

"Me, too!" Natalie and Evie cried together.

"How about you, Honey?" asked Florence.

"I'm not going," she replied quietly.

"What? Why?" Evie cried, in alarm.

Honey shrugged. "It'll be cold and dark there."

"But Honey—" Florence began. Before she could finish, Honey dashed away across the playground.

Just then, Mr Hazelgrove appeared. "Time for class, everyone."

"We'll have to wait till later," Evie whispered to Florence and Natalie. "But we've got to change Honey's mind. We can't have a sleepover without her."

After school, the friends dropped Reggie off at home, then headed for Primrose Meadow.

"Have you really decided not to come to the sleepover, Honey?" asked Evie.

Honey shook her head miserably. "The truth is I can't ask Mum and Dad to let me go," she said. "If I do, Harvey and Albie will find out about the den."

"Wait until they've gone out," suggested Natalie.

"That's the trouble," Honey sighed. "They hardly go out at the moment. They're building a beetle trap and it's taking them ages."

"Could you come up with a different reason for staying out all night?" asked Florence.

They all thought hard. "I've got it!" Honey squeaked. "I'll tell them we're going on an all-night foraging expedition."

Evie frowned. "I'm not sure that will work, Honey."

"Of course it will," insisted Honey. "There's nothing more important than having a full larder for winter. Mum and Dad should be pleased that I'm working so hard."

They headed for Honey's nest and found Mr and Mrs Pennyroyal in the living room with Harvey and Albie. The boys were sticking twigs together to make their trap.

"We're planning an all-night foraging expedition on Saturday," said Honey. "Can I go, please?"

"All night?" repeated Mrs Pennyroyal. "Just the four of you?"

"Yes."

Mr Pennyroyal shook his head. "You won't be able to see where you're going."

"I'll take a lantern," said Honey. She glared at Harvey and Albie, who were pulling faces at her from behind her parents' backs.

"I'm sorry, Honey," said Mr Pennyroyal.

"But Dad..."

"No, Honey. And that's final."

Honey and her friends headed for her bedroom. “That’s that then,” Honey sighed.

“Don’t give up, Honey,” Evie said. “We’ll just have to think of another reason for being out all night.”

“What about camping?” suggested Natalie.

“That should do the trick,” said Evie.

They ran back to the living room. “Can I go camping instead?” Honey asked hopefully.

"It's too cold for camping," said Mrs Pennyroyal. "Why don't you wait until spring?"

"Because that's ages away," said Honey. "We'll take plenty of blankets."

"Don't argue with your mother," Mr Pennyroyal said sternly. "You're not camping at this time of year."

"You'll have to go without me," said Honey, when they were back in her bedroom.

"No way!" cried Evie. "We've got until Saturday to work out a new plan. Let's all think of something tonight, then we can choose the best idea at school tomorrow."

When Mr Hazelgrove called everyone into school next morning, the friends hung back. "It's best to tell the truth about the sleepover, Honey," said Natalie, checking that nobody was near enough to overhear. "Your mum and dad will probably let you go then, but we need to get Harvey and Albie out of the way before you ask."

"I know how to do that!" Evie laughed. "We'll talk about some imaginary secret plan. Harvey and Albie will be so busy trying to overhear us that they won't bother about what you're up to."

"Great idea, Evie!" Florence giggled. "Let's do it after school today, Honey. It'll be a relief to know for sure that our sleepover's still on."

"My mum and dad are out today," sighed Honey. "They've gone to visit friends on the far side of Bluebell Woods and they won't be back till late."

"Tomorrow then," Evie said. She squeezed Honey's paw. "Stop worrying. I'm sure everything will be OK."

Honey forced a smile. "I hope you're right."

Next day, the friends raced round to Honey's nest straight after school, and found Harvey and Albie in the living room, still building their trap. "Hey, listen everyone," Evie said in a loud whisper to her friends. "About our plan..." She was pleased to see Harvey and Albie prick up their ears.

"Why don't we go into Honey's bedroom so we can talk about it in secret?" said Evie. As they went out of the living room, Honey dived into the kitchen where her parents were preparing dinner.

Evie, Florence and Natalie went along the passageway and into Honey's bedroom. As she shut the door, Evie noticed Harvey and Albie tiptoeing after them. "It's working," she whispered. Raising her voice a little, she said, "We mustn't let anybody find out what we're planning."

"Yes," agreed Florence. "They'll only try to stop us."

"Shall I bring the acorns?" said Natalie.

"Yes, and we'll have to find loads of mud," Evie added, trying not to giggle.

They heard whispering outside the door and grinned at each other. The boys must have heard everything and Evie imagined them trying to work out what on earth they were planning. Suddenly, she heard Honey's voice. "What are you doing outside my bedroom?"

"Nothing," said Albie guiltily.

The door opened and Honey came in, beaming. She watched her brothers scampering away, then performed a joyful pirouette. "It worked! I can go!"

"Fantastic!" Evie whooped. She couldn't wait for tomorrow.

Next morning, the friends went round to Natalie's nest and set to work making pasties for their midnight feast. "These are going to be soooo yummy!" Honey exclaimed, as she chopped the carrots.

"My mum's baked us some cookies," said Evie.

"And my dad's got some blankets for us," Florence added.

Natalie went to the larder and brought back four bottles of elderflower cordial. "We can take these," she said.

"We'll never be able to carry everything in one go," said Honey. "Let's take the food and drink to the den first, then come back for our blankets and pyjamas."

"Good idea," they agreed.

As they carried everything out from under the bramble thicket, Reggie appeared. "Can I play with you?" he asked.

"Not now, Reggie," said Evie. "We're a bit busy. But we'll play with you later, when we get back from the woods."

Reggie nodded glumly, and the friends hurried to the Stepping Stones. "I feel so mean, leaving him out," said Evie, as they crossed the Babbling Brook.

"We'll be back soon," Honey said. "There should be time for a game with him before we head off for the sleepover."

As they went into the woods, Reggie ran down to the Stepping Stones. He hopped across quickly, then skipped along the path they'd taken. He was determined not to be left behind.

The friends reached the den and squeezed inside. By the time Reggie reached the ash tree, there was no sign of them and he carried on along the path. Suddenly, he spotted a hazelnut.

"Yummy," he said, picking it up and cracking it open. "Oh look, there's more!" He followed the hazelnut trail deep into the woods, nibbling as he went.

The den was ready for the sleepover. "It looks really homely," said Natalie, gazing around approvingly. They'd brought in armfuls of dried leaves to use as mattresses, and the food was set out ready for the midnight feast.

"If everything's ready we should go and play with Reggie," said Evie.

They hurried back across the Stepping Stones, but there was no sign of the little squirrel. "Let's fetch the rest of our stuff for tonight instead," said Honey.

Evie ran home and packed her pyjamas and some card games in her backpack.

Then she went to say goodbye to her mum and dad. "I'm off now," she said.

"Where's Reggie?" asked Dad.

"I don't know. He was in Primrose Meadow earlier, but he'd gone by the time we came back from our den."

Mr Morningdew stood up and looked out of the window. "I can't see him anywhere."

"I hope he hasn't gone into Bluebell Woods by himself," said Mrs Morningdew. "He doesn't really know his way around." She pulled on her coat. "Let's go and look for him, Rufus."

"I'll get my friends and we'll look, too," said Evie.

Evie rushed to find her friends, who were waiting for her in Primrose Meadows. "Reggie's missing!" she cried. "Will you…?" She broke off as a terrible thought occurred to her. "What if he's gone to Campion Forest to find Oscar?"

"He wouldn't, would he?" gasped Honey. "It's such a long way."

"There's no point getting in a panic," Natalie said, patting Evie's arm. "Let's start searching close to home, and if we don't find him, then we can worry about Campion Forest."

The friends dashed across Primrose Meadow, calling Reggie's name.

Albie came out from under the hedgerow. "What's going on?" he asked.

"We've lost Reggie," said Evie.

"We saw him on the other side of the

Stepping Stones earlier," said Harvey, poking out his head. "He was following you lot."

"Following us?" Evie gasped. "We didn't notice him."

"Run and find Evie's mum and dad, and tell them where you saw him," said Honey.

The boys hurried off, and the friends darted across the Stepping Stones and into Bluebell Woods, calling as they went.

"Reggie must have lost sight of us when we went into the den," said Evie. "He could be anywhere by now."

The friends raced to their den, but there was no sign of Reggie. "Where could he be?" groaned Evie. "He's too little to have gone so far." She blamed herself for not spending more time with her brother. Why hadn't she played with him when he'd asked? Why hadn't she spent more time finding him a friend, instead of setting up the den?

Suddenly, Honey gasped. "You remember that trail of hazelnuts I left when my basket had a hole in it?"

Evie nodded.

"The nuts have gone," said Honey. "Do you think Reggie found them?"

"Maybe," said Florence hopefully, touching her tail three times for luck. "If he did, he'll be heading for the Hazel Grove."

They charged along the path, peering to left and right. "Reggie, where are you?" they shouted at the tops of their voices. In the distance, they could hear Mr and Mrs Morningdew searching, and the woods rang with their calls.

At last, as the friends drew close to the Hazel Grove, they heard an answering call. "I'm here!"

"Reggie!" Evie darted in the direction of his voice and found him crouched behind a clump of grass. "Are you OK?" she asked, hugging him.

"Of course. Except you've ruined my game," he said crossly. "I'm playing hide-and-seek and I've given away my hiding place by calling to you."

"Who are you playing with?" asked Natalie, surprised.

"Me," said Peter, jumping down beside them. "Found you, Reggie!"

Mr and Mrs Morningdew appeared. They were still calling Reggie's name.

"He's here!" shouted Evie.

Wilbur and Alice Morningdew came bounding through the trees. "What's all the excitement about?" asked Wilbur. Then he spotted Evie's mum and dad. "Hello," he cried. "Are you Evie's parents?"

"That's right," they said, surprised.

"I think we're distant cousins," Wilbur said, shaking Mr Morningdew's paw. "I've been looking forward to meeting you."

"I don't want to go home yet," said Reggie. "I want to stay and play with Peter."

Alice smiled. "You'll be able to play together every day soon," she said. "We're moving to your village so Peter can go to school. Evie told us how lovely it is there."

"Fantastic!" cheered Evie. She was overjoyed that it seemed Reggie would have a friend to play with again. "Can we play hide-and-seek with you, boys?" she asked, keen to spend some time with Reggie after the scare they'd had.

"OK," said Reggie. "You be seeker."

"...Forty-nine, fifty. Coming, ready or not!" cried Evie. Uncovering her eyes, she looked round and spotted the tips of Florence's ears sticking up above a tree root. "Found you, Florence."

"I'll help you look for the others," said Florence.

They scoured the woods and discovered Natalie curled into a spiky ball under a pile of leaves. "There you are, Nat!" Evie exclaimed.

Natalie uncurled, yawning and stretching. "What took you so long?" She giggled. "I nearly fell asleep."

Peter and Reggie were hiding together in a hollow between two roots.

"Found you," said Evie. It was great that the two boys seemed to be firm friends already.

They all searched for Honey. Finally, Natalie spotted her thin tail hanging down from a low branch just above her head. Honey was squeezed into the fork between two twigs. Natalie pulled her tail gently. "Got you," she said.

Honey jumped down. "It was a good hiding place, wasn't it? You kept walking underneath without noticing me."

By now the sky was darkening along its eastern edge and the pale moon was already visible.

Mrs Morningdew pulled Evie aside. "Haven't you four got a sleepover to go to?" she asked.

Evie's paw flew to her mouth. "We were having so much fun I almost forgot," she said.

It was nearly dark when the friends arrived at their den with their pyjamas and blankets. They crawled inside and plumped up the piles of dried leaves, then spread out the blankets. Honey lit the lantern and the candle flame flickered brightly, lighting every corner of the den. They then changed into their pyjamas, giggling as they bumped into each other in the small space.

Evie, Florence and Honey chattered excitedly about the night ahead and the midnight feast. "Are you OK, Nat?" asked Florence. "You seem a bit quiet."

Natalie shivered. "I don't think I like it here at night. It's spooky."

"No, it's not," said Evie. "It's cosy." She sat down next to Natalie and took her paw.

"I want to go home," said Natalie.

"Think of the midnight feast, Nat," said Honey. "And of waking up here in the morning, all of us together."

"I've got a joke for you," said Florence. "Why do bees have sticky hair?"

"I don't know," Evie said.

"Because they use honeycombs."

They all laughed.

"How can you tell which end of a worm is the head?" Evie asked. She grinned at their blank faces. "Tickle the middle and see which end laughs."

"This is brilliant fun," sighed Honey. "I'm so glad I could come. Are you feeling better yet, Nat?"

"Much better, thanks."

"How about a game of snap?" suggested Florence, taking out a pack of cards.

They played games until it was time for their midnight feast.

"Carrot and garlic pasties!" cried Honey, handing them out. She took a big bite. "Food always tastes better when you're somewhere exciting."

At last, they all began to yawn.

"I'm tired," said Evie. "It's been quite a day."

"Me, too," said Florence, rubbing her eyes. "Shall we go to bed?"

"I think so!" agreed Honey, yawning again. "How about it, Nat?"

"Yes, please," Natalie nodded.

Florence blew out the lantern, then they crawled under their blankets and lay side by side, gazing at the stars twinkling through the crack in the tree trunk.

"This is the best secret den ever," said Florence sleepily.

"And I bet we'll have lots more adventures here," Evie added happily.

Have you read?

Bluebell Woods
Liss Norton
Honey's Summer Ball